THE CREAM OF CHINESE CULTURE

PEKING OPERA

The Cream of Chinese Culture
Peking Opera

Compiled by Yi Bian

FOREIGN LANGUAGES PRESS

First Edition 2005
Second Printing 2007

ISBN 978-7-119-03697-7
Foreign Languages Press, Beijing, China, 2005

Published by Foreign Languages Press
24 Baiwanzhuang Road, Beijing 100037, China
Website: http://www.flp.com.cn
Email Addresses: Info@flp.com.cn
Sales@flp.com.cn

Distributed by China International Book Trading Corporation
35 Chegongzhuang Xilu, Beijing 100044, China
P.O.Box 399, Beijing, China

Printed in the People's Republic of China

Contents

Foreword

前言

Formation of Peking Opera

Peking opera is regarded as China's national opera and is the most popular and widespread opera in the country. It is generally believed that Peking opera developed from several ancient local operas during the mid - and late 19th century. In 1790, the 55th year of the Qing Dynasty Emperor Qianlong's reign, the Sanqing Anhui Opera Troupe moved from Anhui Province to Beijing to perform in the celebrations to - mark Emperor Qianlong's 80th birthday. Later, three more Anhui opera troupes - the Sixi, Chuntai, Hechun troupes - also came to perform in Beijing. Together with Sanqing, they were referred to as the Four Anhui Opera Troupes. Each troupe had its own characteristic way of performing. The troupes and the Han opera performers from Hubei with whom they were working had a mutual influence on one another. The performers also borrowed some plays, melodies and performing techniques from Kunqu and Shaanxi opera, drew on some folk tunes, and showed

A folk theater

a greater and greater Beijing influence in terms of the lyrics, recitative and rhyme, gradually developing what is now Peking opera.

Peking opera is a comprehensive art that has singing, recitation, acting and acrobatics (dancing) at its core. Feelings and ideas are often expressed through symbolic motions, and the unique format has developed over long years of performance. Using its standardized yet flexible format, many Peking opera artists have created a lot of vivid, touching characters with distinct personalities, thus helping Peking opera develop and prosper.

A map of the old city of Beijing

❶ The Outer City

❷ The Inner City

❸ The Imperial City

❹ The Forbidden City

A performance in a teahouse during the Qing Emperor Guangxu's reign (1875—1908)

4

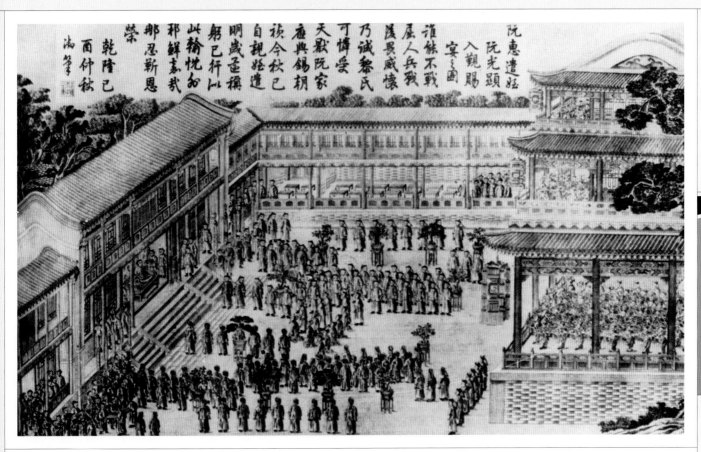

阮惠遣姪
阮光顯
入覲賜
宴之圖
誰能不戰
展人兵我
護畏咸懷
乃誠黎民
可博受
天戰阮家
庶興錫朝
諗今秋已
自視姪遣
明歲盂稱
躬已行以
此翰忱勿
邪鮮嘉裁
那恩新恩
榮
乾隆己
酉仲秋
御筆

The Qing Emperor Qianlong (r.1736—1795) watching an opera at his mountain summer resort

Peking opera takes its name from the city of Beijing, where it developed. It was formerly called *pihuang* (after *xipi* and *erhuang*, the two main types of melody in Peking opera), Beiping opera (after an old name of Beijing) and National opera, among other names.

A theater building

Beijing's South-Facing Gate (Zhengyangmen)

Types of Roles

Peking opera is a theatrical art that incorporates singing, dancing, acting and acrobatics. But what we see on the Peking opera stage does not imitate real life. For example, Peking opera uses special imagery in the creation of characters. All roles are classified according to sex, personality, age, profession and social status. *Hangdang* is the general term for role types in Peking opera. As we all know, there are four types of role in Peking opera today - namely, the *sheng* (male role), *dan* (female role), *jing* (painted face) and *chou* (clown). The *sheng* is the male protagonist, the *dan* the female protagonist, the *jing* a male supporting figure with distinct characteristics, and *chou* a comic or negative figure or foil for the protagonist. The four role types are a result of the large variety of roles from earlier stages in the history of Peking opera being combined and reduced.

A scene from the cour play *Reed Catkins River* (*Luhua He*)

8

The *sheng* role type: Ma Lianliang as Qiao Xuan in *At the Sweet Dew Temple* (*Ganlu Si*)

The *dan* role type: Mei Lanfang as Yang Yuhuan in *The Drunken Beauty* (*Guifei Zuijiu*)

The *jing* role type: Qiu Shengrong as Yao Qi in *General Yao Qi* (*Yao Qi*) (Performer: Qi Xiaoyun)

The four basic role types have their subdivisions, each with its own specialties and techniques. For example, the *sheng* role is divided into elderly (*laosheng*), young (*xiaosheng*), military (*wusheng*), red-faced (*hongsheng*) and young boy (*wawasheng*) roles, and the elderly male role can be further divided into singing, acting and martial *laosheng* roles, and so on. The role types cover all the characters on stage, and every actor or actress specializes in a particular role type.

The role types in Peking opera have been artistically refined to categorize, systematize and standardize the myriad images in the complex life of society according to the practical requirements of opera performance. The role types distinguish the characters' inner traits, expressed through appearance. Thus came about Peking opera's unique system of imagery, which functions as a framework in this integrated theatrical art and distinguishes Peking opera from other types of opera.

Based on the role types, a complete set of standards has been formed for aspects such as costumes and facial makeup. These aspects and the classification of role types supplement each other, both being very important in the creation of characters and demonstrating the full beauty of Peking opera.

The *chou* role type: Xiao Changhua (left) as Tang Qin in *From Trial of the Severed Head to the Killing of Tang Qin* (*Shen Tou Ci Tang*)

Costume

The costumes in Peking opera are based on Ming Dynasty fashions, also borrowing from the fashions of the Tang, Song, Yuan and Qing dynasties and modern times. They are as diverse as the roles: civil and military, male and female, and so on. Traditional Peking opera plays are mainly based on historical events, reflecting life in each dynasty, with characters ranging from emperors, generals and ministers to the common people. Characters from different dynasties and with different social statuses wear different costumes on stage, each having its own rules of dress.

Characters from *The Legend of Yang Yuhuan* (*Taizhen Waizhuan*)

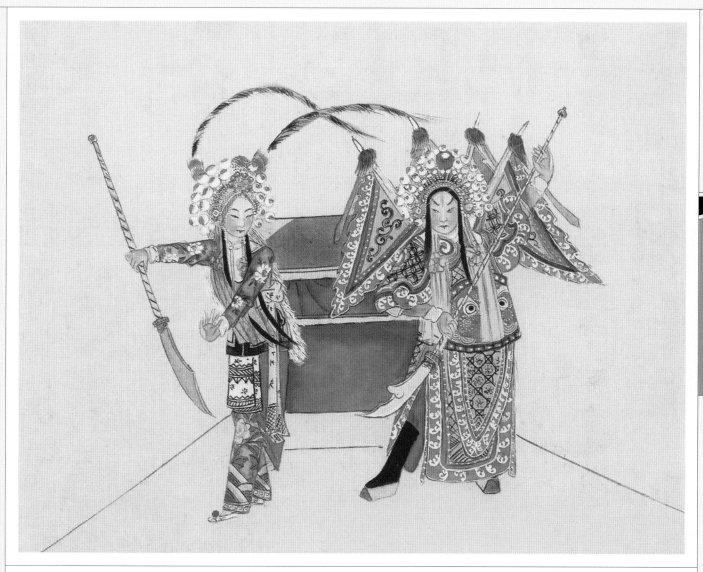

Characters from *The Blue Stone Mountain* (*Qingshi Shan*)

Laodan

Huadan

Wudan

As the role types came into being, the costumes were classified and standardized accordingly. Each role type has a relatively fixed form of costume. Different role types and different subtypes within the same role type are distinguished by their costumes. For example, there are various colorful costumes for female (*dan*) roles. Some roles of elderly women (*laodan*) with higher social status use ceremonial dress, such as a woman's *mang* (a robe with a python design), on formal occasions. The young women (*huadan*) roles use close-fitting, simpler dresses to show their liveliness and beauty. The roles of military women (*wudan*) use armor (*kao*), which show their valiant bearing. The classification and standardization of Peking opera costumes, in line with the classification of role types, meet the need of stylized performance.

Facial Makeup

Facial makeup is another important means of character creation in Peking opera. A special Chinese form of makeup, it expresses the characters' personalities and traits, as well as the role type to which the characters belong, in two ways. One way is how the face is painted in certain colors. For example, a red-faced character is valiant, loyal and positive, while yellow-faced and white-faced characters are sinister, treacherous and negative. The other way is how lines and patterns are drawn on the face. For example, a distorted face, drawn with asymmetrical lines, generally represents a vicious villain or accomplice or someone whose face has been wounded.

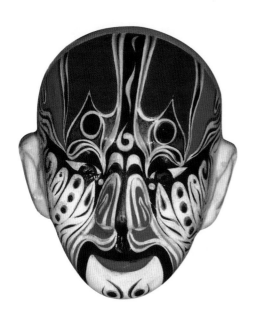

Painted faces

Painted faces

The classification of role types makes it possible for actors and actresses to train according to the requirements of their own type of role, quickly mastering the special singing, acting and other techniques, ready to perform on stage. The role types, costumes and facial makeup enable the audience to perceive the different characters clearly and directly. When they are familiar with the role types and their corresponding costumes and facial makeup, the members of the audience are able to distinguish the characteristics of the different role types and understand the characters. This gives rise to strong theatrical effects in a performance, and the audience's interest is more easily aroused. For example, when a certain character appears on stage, the audience will recognize the role type by the costume, facial makeup and other information such as how the character moves and the melodies that he or she sings. Various styles and different traits were thus established for Peking opera characters, and the audience's attention is drawn to the plot and performance through the simplest and most economical means. This is one of the major artistic advantages of Peking opera.

Schools and Plays

Peking opera's more than two centuries of development have seen the appearance of many schools, which are named after actors, such as the Mei school and the Cheng school. This is because Peking opera is a theatrical system with the actors' performance at its core, and Peking opera's artistic achievements are mainly due to the actors. The development of the various schools of Peking opera is closely related to the classification of role types. We could even say that schools have emerged on the basis of this classification. Each role type has its representative artists, whose artistic traits predominate in each school. For example, the Tan school specializes in the role of the elderly man (*laosheng*) and is named after the actor Tan Xinpei, who was famous for this type of role; and the Mei school, specializing in the role of the woman (*dan*), was established by the actor Mei Lanfang, who was famous for this type of role.

In Peking opera's more than 200 years on stage, over 1,000 plays have been written, both traditional plays and new plays written by various schools as their representative plays. Many of the Peking opera plays have been popular with audiences for generations.

A playbill from 1913

The playbill of a Mei Lanfang performance in Hong Kong in 1922

The program of a court play from the Qing Dynasty Emperor Guangxu's reign

Musical Instruments and Orchestras

The many instruments used in Peking opera fall into two main categories. One kind includes wind instruments, such as the bamboo flute (*di*), reed pipe (*sheng*) and *suona* horn, and stringed instruments such as the Peking opera fiddle (*jinghu*), the *erhu* two-stringed fiddle, the four-stringed moon-shaped Chinese mandolin (*yueqin*), and the smaller *sanxian*, a three-stringed plucked instrument. The other kind comprises percussion instruments, such as the drum (*gu*), bamboo clappers (*ban*), gong (*luo*), cymbals (*bo*) and bell (*zhong*).

Musicians in the old days playing in front of a curtain

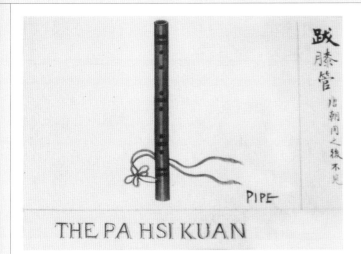

跋膝管 唐朝用之後不見

PIPE

THE PA HSI KUAN

玉笙 漢時有之後不見

JADE PANDEAN PIPES

THE YU SHENG

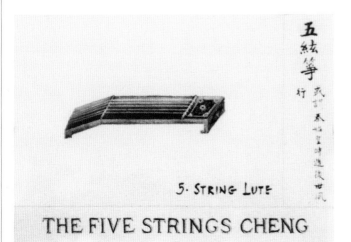

五絃筝 行 武帝秦始皇時造後世亂

5. STRING LUTE

THE FIVE STRINGS CHENG

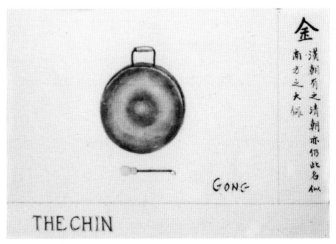

金 漢朝有之清朝亦仍此名似 南方之大饒

GONG

THE CHIN

Musical instruments

The Peking opera orchestra is generally called *changmian*, which originally means "facing the stage." In the early years, the stage was mostly square, and there were tables, chairs and musical instruments right in front of the curtain hanging over the rear half of the stage, where the musicians sat during the performance. This seating arrangement for the orchestra was called *changmian*, and this word later became the term for the orchestra itself.

There are orchestras for "gentle shows" (*wenchang*) and orchestras for shows with acrobatic fighting (*wuchang*). In the kind of shows which are mostly singing, the accompanying music is played with wind and stringed instruments, so such instruments are also called *wenchang* ("civilian stage"). The percussion instruments, which produce strong and rhythmic music, are often used to accompany acrobatic fighting and are known as *wuchang* ("military stage").

Vocal Music

Vocal music (*changqiang*) comprises the tunes and the types of meter for which they are pertinent. Chinese opera singing is divided into metrical and versified styles. The main singing style in Peking opera is metrical, with lyrics similar to *lüshi* poetry, each line consisting of seven, 10 or more characters, and the final characters of most lines rhyming with each other. The lines are in pairs, the first of which ends with an oblique-tone character, and the second with a level-tone character.

The main musical styles of Peking opera are *xipi* and *erhuang*. *Xipi* features high-pitched, lively tunes, while *erhuang* features steady, deep tunes. Each style has various kinds of meter, which are called *banshi*. Peking opera's different *banshi* express different feelings and meet the needs of the different plots of different plays.

A traditional stage setting of a table and two chairs

The scene of sightseeing round the lake in
A Tale of the White Snake (*Baishe Zhuan*)

Setting and Props

The scenery on the Peking opera stage, usually in the *xieyi* style (a freehand expres- sionist style) or symbolic style, is mainly for enhancing and adding to the play. A com- monly seen traditional setting consists of one table and two chairs, which are ar- ranged in different positions to suggest different meanings.

Among the myriad props of Peking opera are military weapons, such as swords, spears and hammers, and everyday objects such as rows, horsewhips, writing brushes, ink, paper and inkstones. There are symbolic objects, such as a white square banner with ripple patterns to represent waves, and a pair of square yellow flags each with a painting of a wheel, which the actor holds in his hands while moving as if he was pulling a chariot.

Many modern methods are now used to enhance the atmosphere on stage and add to the play.

The stage setting for Mei Lanfang's 1928 performance in Guangzhou

Theater Buildings

The Chinese word *xilou* is a name given to the place where a play is staged. After many years of development, theater construction entered its prime during the Qing Dynasty for various reasons, including the fondness of that dynasty's emperors of watching plays. As Peking opera emerged, theaters developed even more quickly, with imperial theaters being

Inside Tianjin's Guangming Grand Theater

among the largest in scale.

Chinese theater buildings can be classified into three main types: modern European-style theaters, imperial theaters and folk theaters (*minjian xilou*). The first type is called *juchang* or *juyuan*. The last type is usually called *xitai* (stage) because this kind of theater is relatively small, sometimes being just a simple thatched shed. Imperial theaters are used only for large-scale performances. The theaters used for ordinary performances in imperial palaces are also called *xitai*. Most extant theaters are of the modern European style. Of the traditional Chinese-style theaters, imperial theaters have been well preserved, while most folk theaters have fallen into disrepair and disappeared. We can only see some of them in paintings from the past.

The Pavilion of Cheerful Melodies (Changyin Ge), a theater in the Forbidden City's Palace of Peace and Longevity (Ningshou Gong)

Picture of an opera performance in a rural area in the late Qing Dynasty, painted in 1875

As a comprehensive theatrical art, Peking opera combines singing, speech, acting, acrobatics, makeup and stage scenery into a harmonious whole, with an entire set of standards and formats that has been developed during long years of theatrical practice. The aspects mentioned above are basic components of the standards and formats but can never cover the extensiveness and profundity of Peking opera.

Mural showing opera scenes in Beijing's Jingzhong Temple

With their superb performing skills, famous Peking opera actors have developed various schools and different styles. Peking opera deserves its reputation as the "national opera" in every respect. With a rich store of cultural heritage and a rich repertoire of plays, Peking opera is a treasure-house of Chinese operatic art and a shining pearl of Eastern art.

Liu Zhen and Song Bo

Institute of Traditional Operas, Chinese Academy of Arts

Sheng – Male Roles

Sheng or male roles constitute one of the basic role types in Peking opera. Many talented people have thrived in this type of role.

The sheng roles are generally positive and can be divided into laosheng (elderly men), wusheng (military men), xiaosheng (young men), wawasheng (boys), and hongsheng (red-faced men).

With the exception of the red-faced men and the military men with their painted faces, the sheng characters usually wear light makeup and look refined and handsome.

1 Laosheng – Elderly Men

Laosheng refers to male characters who are middle-aged or older. They are also called *zhengsheng* (respectable men) because the characters are usually serious and dignified.

Laosheng characters are also called *xusheng* (bearded men) because they all wear beards. The beard is often black and in three wisps. Some beards are gray or white. There are also full beards.

Laosheng characters often appear in light makeup, wearing beards. They move with dignity, and sing and speak with their real voices. Different characters require different costumes and different ways of performing.

There are civilian *laosheng* and military *laosheng*. In terms of how they are performed, they are divided into singing *laosheng*, acting *laosheng* and military *laosheng* who both sing and do acrobatics.

There are various schools of *laosheng*. Of the many famous *laosheng* actors, some are good at singing, some good at acting or

Laosheng: Lü Boshe (left) and Chen Gong (center) in *The Capture and Release of Cao Cao* (*Zhuo Fang Cao*)

Black Tripartite Beard

A black three-wisped beard

Black Full Beard

A black full beard

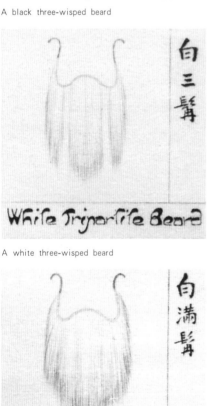

White Tripartite Beard

A white three-wisped beard

White Full Beard

A white full beard

acrobatics, and some at all three. The famous performer Tan Xinpei (1847-1917), dubbed the "King of Actors," was excellent at singing, acting and acrobatics.

A black full beard

Tan Xinpei (right) as Cao Fu in *South Gate to Heaven (Nantian Men)*

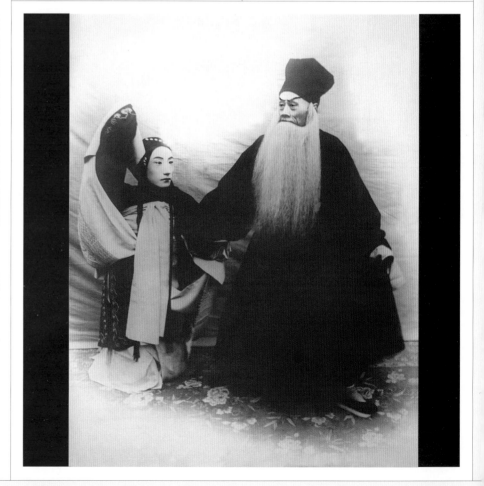

Singing *laosheng*: The character Zhuge Liang
in *Borrowing the East Wind* (*Jie Dongfeng*)

Acting a *laosheng* part: The character Song Shijie
in *Four Newly Appointed Officials* (*Si Jinshi*)

Civilian *Laosheng*

Singing *laosheng* and dancing *laosheng* both fall into the category of civilian *laosheng*. Singing *laosheng* characters are mostly of a higher status, such as emperors, virtuous ministers, loyal court officials, scholar-generals and scholars. The actors express the characters' personalities, thoughts and feelings through intensive singing. Acting *laosheng* characters are often of a lower social status, such as petty officials, storekeepers and servants. Their feelings and traits are expressed through complicated, difficult movements and long speeches.

Costumes

Civilian *laosheng* characters, being generally serious and dignified, often wear formal attire, such as *mang* (python-design robes) and *guanyi* (officials' gowns), on formal occasions and wear casual clothes, such as *pei* (capes) and *zhezi*, or *xuezi* as it is popularly known to people in theatrical circles (robes that overlap at the front), at home or on informal occasions.

Mang — Python-design Robes

Mang are formal robes worn by characters of high status such as emperors, kings, generals and ministers on official, serious occasions. The characters always wear a jade belt with the mang robe to stress the solemnity of the occasion.

The Chinese word mang means python. In Chinese feudal society, the dragon symbolized the emperor, and dragon-design robes were exclusive to the emperor. The dragon-design robes that emperor characters wore on stage were referred to as python-design (mang) because no one dared to call them by their real name.

A mang is generally long and made of satin, with patterns embroidered with gold and silver threads and threads of other colors.

A yellow *mang*

The Blue Mang

A white *mang*   A man´s *mang* robe

There are mang for men and mang for women. Those for men mainly have a dragon pattern. Some are embroidered with brilliant, solemnly colorful circular clouds, the sun, the moon, the sea and breaking waves or other patterns.

Men's mang differ in color according to the character's status and personality. For example, characters such as emperors, kings and princes wear yellow mang. Characters immediately below the emperor, such as aristocrats, ministers, marshals, imperial envoys and emperors' sons-in-law, wear red mang. Young, handsome characters, such as Zhou Yu and Lü Bu, wear white mang. Boorish, bold characters wear black mang. Most jing (painted-face) roles wear black mang to go with their facial makeup. Characters such as Bao Zheng, Zhang Fei and Xiang Yu, who have dark complexions, wear black mang.

Guanyi — Official's Gowns

Guanyi are gowns for lower-ranking civilian officials. They are worn on serious occasions, often with a jade belt.

There are guanyi for men and guanyi for women but they are mainly worn by men.

Guanyi are similar to mang in style, except that they are made of plain satin, without embroidered patterns such as dragons and clouds. The only decorations are one square patch of embroidery on the front and another on the back, known as buzi.

Like mang, guanyi come in different colors for officials of different levels. Generally, characters wearing red guanyi are higher-ranking officials than those in blue, and the lowest-ranking officials wear black guanyi.

A blue *guanyi*

蓝官衣

WORN BY COURTIERS STILL LOWER IN RANK

The Blue Official Clothing

A man's *guanyi* gown

A waman's *guanyi*

女红官衣

WORN BY WIVES OF DISTINGUISHED SCHOLARS & OF HIGH OFFICIALS

The Female Red Official Clothing

Pei — Capes

Pei are casual clothing worn by high-ranking officials or rich people at home.

Men's pei are usually long, reaching the top of the feet, while women's pei are shorter, reaching below the knees and showing the skirt underneath.

Pei are made of satin and usually decorated with embroidered patterns, such as dragons, phoenixes, flowers and herbs.

Pei mainly come in yellow, red and blue. Yellow pei, like yellow mang, are exclusive to emperors and empresses. Newlyweds wear red pei, as do officials on first taking office.

Yellow *pei* are exclusive to emperors and empresses in Peking opera, so they are also called imperial *pei* (*huangpei*). This is Liu Xiu in *Beating Golden Bricks* (*Da Jinzhuan*).

A woman's *pei*

A man's *pei* cape

黄帔

WORN AS LESS FORMAL COSTUMES BY EMPEROR OR CROWN PRINCE

The Yellow Pei

女红帔

WORN BY YOUNG LADIES

The Female Red Pei

35

Zhezi — Robes That Overlap at the Front

Zhezi, or xuezi as it is popularly known to people in theatrical circles, are the most common form of casual clothing in Peking opera. Men and women, elderly people and children, rich and poor, and people of high or low social status may all wear them.

Fan Zhongyu in *Asking the Woodsman* (*Wen Qiao Nao Fu*)

A man's floral-pattern *zhezi* (*xuezi*) robe

紅軟褶子

WORN BENEATH CEREMONIAL ROBES & AS ORDINARY COSTUME BY YOUNG MEN OF THE NOBILITY

The Red Soft Hsü-eh-tzu

A man's plain black *zhezi* (*xuezi*)

紅硬素褶子

WORN AS ORDINARY COSTUME BY THE EMPEROR

The Red Hard plain Hsüeh-tzu

Women's zhezi (xuezi) are shorter than men's, showing the skirt underneath.

There are two kinds of zhezi (xuezi) in terms of style: embroidered and plain.

Zhezi (xuezi) are mostly made of satin, with a hard texture so that they look neat with embroidery. All role types can wear embroidered zhezi (xuezi), which can be of any color. There are no specific requirements or rules as long as the patterns look beautiful.

Different colors of plain zhezi (xuezi) indicate different types of characters. For example, those wearing blue zhezi (xuezi) are mostly scholars, while those wearing black zhezi (xuezi) are mostly poor and unsuccessful people at the bottom of the social ladder.

A woman's floral-pattern *zhezi* (*xuezi*)

女红裙子

WORN ON HAPPY OCCASIONS BY YOUNG LADIES OF THE NOBILITY

The Female Red Hsü-ch-tzu

Liu Mengmei in *The Peony Pavilion* (*Mudan Ting*)

Wulaoshang – Elderly Military Men Roles

Wulaosheng are divided into *changkao laosheng* or *kaoba laosheng* (armor-clad warriors) and *jianyi laosheng* (warriors dressed as archers).

The term *kaoba laosheng* refers to the role of armor-clad elderly men who carry weapons and are skilled at martial arts.

The attire of archers originated from the Qing Dynasty. People during that time, especially Manchu people, were good horse riders and archers. The clothing served as both an official robe and their hunting attire. It is tight-fitting, girdled at the waist, and has vents at the front and back below the waist to enable ease of movement.

Zhou Yu in an archer's robe in *Meeting of Heroes* (*Qunying Hui*)

A dragon-patterned archer's robe

Armor-clad *laosheng*: Tan Xinpei as Huang Zhong in *Yangping Pass* (*Yangping Guan*)

Kao —Armor

Kao is a kind of Peking opera costume but the word also refers to the armor that ancient soldiers wore on the battlefield. The real armor was made of leather or iron, but the costume is very different and more beautiful.

Kao is made of plain satin in various colors. Its embroidered scales in gold, silver and other colors give it a brilliant appearance.

White *kao* armor

Kao armor

WORN ON DUTY BY VALIANT YOUNG GENERALS

The White Kao

WORN ON DUTY BY FEROCIOUS WARRIORS

The Black Kao

Black *kao* armor

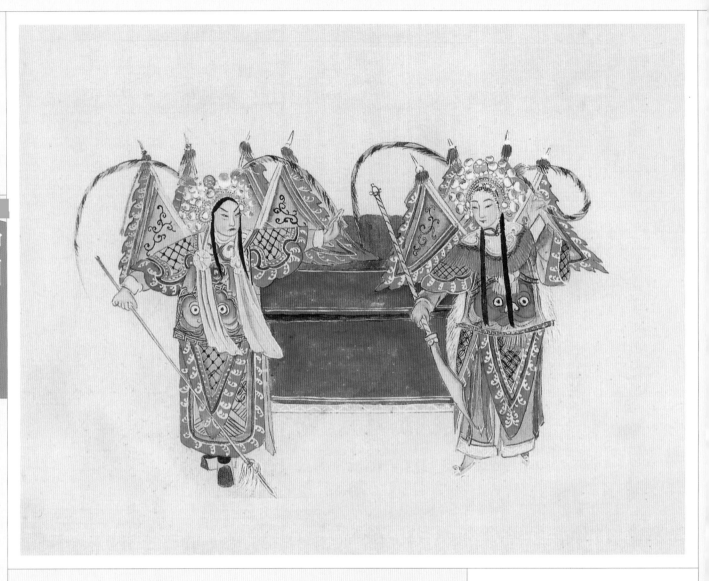

A kao consists of a front part and back part. On the back part are four triangular flags with embroidered dragon patterns in different colors. A colorful ribbon is attached to each flag. When the actor moves, the flags and ribbons flutter behind him, making his movements look more elegant and beautiful. There are no such flags on the real suits of armor. They are included in the costume as decorations to bring out the general's gallantry, show the performer's skills, and add beauty to the dance movements.

Characters from *Marriage Predestined on Horseback* (*Ma Shang Yuan*)

Hongsheng – Red-faced Men Roles

Hongsheng is a special role type under the category of *sheng* (male roles). It is a form of *laosheng* (elderly man role) with red facial makeup. The few such characters include Guan Yu and Zhao Kuangyin. Such characters used to be played by actors specializing in *jing* (painted-face roles), so the characters were known as *hongjing* (red painted-face roles). Later, the parts were played by actors specializing in *laosheng* (elderly man roles) and *wusheng* (warrior roles), so this type of role is now called *hongsheng*.

Hongsheng actors are generally required to have a solid grounding in martial arts. Their movements and postures on stage differ from those of ordinary warrior roles. These actors need special training.

The Peking opera artist Wang Hongshou (1850-1925) was a famous *hongsheng* actor, reputedly the best. He was especially good at playing Guan Yu. *Huarong Pass* (*Huarong Dao*) and *Guan Yu Floods Seven Armies* (*Shuiyan Qijun*) are representative of his works.

Red-faced *sheng*: Guan Yu (center) in *Huarong Pass* (*Huarong Dao*)

2 Wusheng Warrior Roles

Wusheng characters are seasoned, valiant generals and forest outlaws.

There are armor-clad warriors (*changkao wusheng*) and warriors who wear jackets and trousers (*duanda wusheng*).

Changkao Wusheng – Armor-Clad Warriors

Changkao wusheng actors play gallant generals clad in armor who carry weapons and fight on battlefields.

They usually wear a suit of armor, a helmet and thick-soled boots, and generally carry a long-handled weapon.

As well as having excellent martial arts skills, they are required to move and pose in an elegant, steady and stately way, to show the grace and gallantry of a general. In some plays, fine acting, singing and speaking skills are also required.

The great Peking opera master Yang Xiaolou (1877-1938) specialized in *wusheng*. He was especially good at playing armor-clad warriors.

Armor-clad *wusheng*

Headgear

In Peking opera, the actors' headgear falls into four categories: helmets, crowns, hats and kerchiefs. Their different textures and styles indicate the different identities, social positions, trades and ages of the various characters.

Generals wear helmets in battle to protect their heads. The helmets are usually hard inside, and decorated with small woolen

Armor-clad *wusheng*: Yang Xiaolou as Gan Ning in *Gan Ning Raids the Wei Camp with a Hundred Cavalrymen* (*Gan Ning Bai Qi Jie Wei Ying*)

帅盔

COMMANDER-IN-CHIEF
APPOINTED FROM THE RANK OF SCHOLARS

A commander-in-chief's helmet

白夫子盔

YAO FEI & CHAO YÜN

A helmet

方翅纱帽

OFFICIALS OF THE FIRST RANK

An official's gauze hat

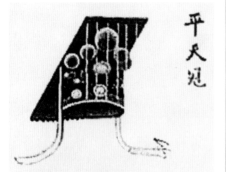

平天冠

EMPEROR ON CEREMONIAL OCCASIONS

A flat—topped crown

九龙冠

EMPEROR AND PRINCES
ON ORDINARY OCCASIONS

A nine—dragon crown

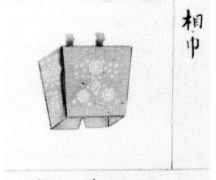

相巾

PRIME MINISTER
ON ORDINARY OCCASIONS

A civilian official's hat

bobbles and beads.

Crowns, which are hard, are worn on cer-emonial occasions. They include the emperor's flat-topped crown and nine-dragon crown, the purple crown of young princes, and the phoe-nix crown of empresses.

Hats and kerchiefs are everyday wear. They come in various styles, soft and hard.

Crowns, hard inside, are worn on cer-emonial occasions, such as the emperor's flat-topped crown and nine-dragon crown, young princes' purple crown, and the empresses' phoenix crown.

Hats and kerchiefs are common daily wear. They are in various styles, with a soft or hard inside.

文生巾

YOUNGER SCHOLARS

A scholar's hat

武生巾

FIGHTERS OF PROVED VALOR

A hat for generals and heroes

Boots

The boots used are mainly thick-soled ones for officials, usually men. The thick soles are meant to make the actors look taller to match the loose, exaggerated costumes such as the mang robes and kao armor.

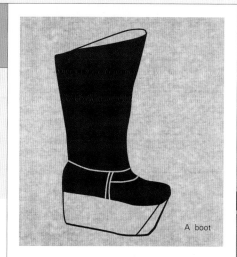

A boot

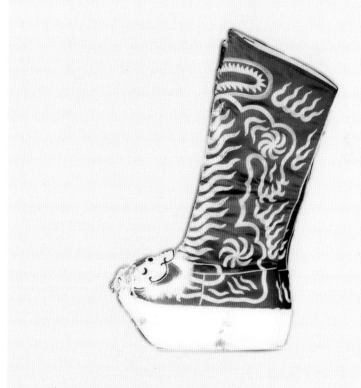

A patterned boots

Shoes

Shoes are for ordinary people. They are decorated for the costumes but bear no special signs.

Women characters usually wear colorful shoes decorated with embroidery and tassels on the front of the uppers.

Su San wearing embroidered shoes in *Escorting the Woman Prisoner* (*Nü Qijie*)

Duanda Wusheng (Warrior in Jackets and Trousers)

The *duanda wusheng* characters are mostly heroes, chivalrous men and swordsmen or local bullies and bandits. They travel at night and ambush people or climb roofs and scale walls, so they wear jackets and trousers, and use short weapons. They are excellent at martial arts and acrobatics, moving swiftly and sturdily.

The jackets and trousers of Peking opera actors are tight-fitting and convenient for brisk movement and fighting. Military clown roles (*wuchou*) also wear jackets and trousers. The jackets and trousers are in two main styles: *kuai* and *bao*.

Wusheng in jacket and trousers: Gai Jiaotian as Wu Song in *Wu Song Fights a Tiger* (*Wu Song Da Hu*)

Kuai Jackets and *Kuai* Trousers

Kuai jackets and kuai trousers may have been designed based on the suits of clothes used for traveling at night described in martial arts novels. The jacket features lines of densely arranged white Chinese-style buttons along the underside of the sleeves and the center at the front. The trousers are black.

快衣

WORN BY FIGHTERS

The Kuai I

A *kuai* jacket

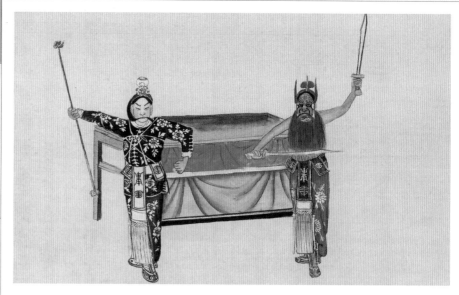

Characters in *kuai* jackets in *White-Water Beach* (*Baishui Tan*)

Characters in *kuai* jackets in *Yanyang Tower* (*Yanyang Lou*)

48

Bao Jackets and Bao Trousers

These are tight-fitting, as if wrapped around the body. They are also called yingxiong yi (heroes' clothes), meaning they are the clothes of chivalrous swordsmen, upright men and heroic forest outlaws.

The jacket features a three-layer silk skirt at the bottom decorated with embroidery. The skirt is called zoushui ("flowing") because it looks like waves.

Bao jacket: Ren Tanghui in *Where Three Roads Meet* (San Cha Kou)

花英雄衣

WORN BY WARRIORS WHEN ENGAGED IN PRIVATE BRAWLS, OR IN FIGHTING FOREIGNERS

The Flowered Ying Hsüng I

古銅色英雄衣

WORN BY OLDER WARRIORS OF THE ABOVE MENTIONED TYPE

The Bronze Ying Hsüng I

A *bao* jacket

49

Magua —
Mandarin Jacket

Characters in jackets and trousers often wear magua (mandarin jackets) on top.

The magua is a Qing Dynasty jacket but, in Peking opera, characters of all dynasties may wear it.

A magua is generally a traveler's coat, worn over an archer's attire. It may also be worn during battles that are not very fierce.

馬褂

WORN AS EVERYDAY JACKET BY EMPEROR & OTHERS WHILE TRAVELLING

A *magua* jacket

An actor in a *magua* jacket

Kaichang—Overcoat

The kaichang *is a casual overcoat worn* by generals in Peking opera.

Characters wearing kaichang *usually wear battle clothes underneath, such as an archer's attire, tight-fitting short jackets and short pants. They will open the front of the overcoat at any time to show the battle clothes, which is a gesture of gallantry and valor or a way of bringing out the tense atmosphere before a battle. They can remove the overcoat whenever necessary before going into battle.*

Li Shaochun as the Monkey King in *Wreaking Havoc in Heaven* (Danao Tiangong)

In addition to the characters mentioned above, *wusheng* actors also play deities and spirits. For example, a *wusheng* actor plays the Monkey King Sun Wukong in the play *Wreaking Havoc in Heaven (Danao Tiangong)*.

The Peking opera performer Gai Jiaotian (1888-1971) was renowned as an excellent *duanda wusheng* actor. A diligent man throughout his life, he never stopped exercising, neither in the cold of winter nor the heat of summer. Even at the age of 70, he was able to somersault on a table and land without making a sound, showing his profound martial arts grounding.

WORN AS ORDINARY COSTUMES BY PRIME MINISTERS & YOUNG GENERALS

The White Kai Chang

A white *kaichang* overcoat

WORN AS ORDINARY COSTUME BY FEROCIOUS WARRIORS

The Black Kai Chang

A black *kaichang* overcoat

Gai Jiaotian as Huang Tianba in *Ferocious Tiger Village* (*E Hu Cun*)

3 Xiaosheng – Young Man Roles

those of elderly men.

The performer Yu Zhenfei (1902-93) specialized in *xiaosheng* characters and was famous for his scholarly grace on stage.

One branch of the *xiaosheng* role type is called *qiongsheng* (roles of unfortunate, impoverished scholars). Such characters mostly wear *fuguiyi* (robes of fortune).

Xiaosheng: Robust and handsome young man

Xiaosheng roles are those of young men in Peking opera. They are clean-shaven and look fine and handsome.

The most distinctive feature of a *xiaosheng* performance is the combination of real and false voices in the singing and speaking. The false voice is generally sharper, thin and highly pitched to sound young and distinguish the characters of young men from

Yu Zhenfei as Zhao Chong in *Unexpected Reunion* (*Qi Shuang Hui*)

Fuguiyi — Robes of Fortune

The fuguiyi is a casual costume in Peking opera. It is basically a zhezi (xuezi) (robe that overlaps at the front) with many small silk patches of various colors to show that it is a heavily patched rag. This kind of costume is usually worn by poverty-stricken, depressed characters. It is known as a "robe of fortune" because, at length, fortune will deliver these characters from their bad situation.

A fuguiyi robe

Fan Ju in Gift of a Silk Robe (Zeng Tipao) is a poor scholar who wears a fuguiyi robe

A page boy in Romance of the Western Chamber (Xixiang Ji)

4 Wawasheng — Boy Roles

Wawasheng actors play boys. They often wear a boy's wig and chayi ("tea clothes").

Unlike xiaosheng actors, wawasheng actors sing and speak with their real voices but in a different way from laosheng actors. Their singing technique is special and combines sheng and dan techniques. The actors are required to express the naivety of children. As it is hard to find child actors, petite actresses often play such roles.

A boy's hairstyle

A chayi robe

Chayi — "Tea Clothes"

The Peking opera costume chayi is a short blue cotton zhezi (xuezi) robe.

Plain in color and simple in style, the chayi is the costume of waiters, woodsmen and fishermen, as well as of children. It is worn by people in the lower strata of society.

Dan – Female Roles

旦

Dan roles make up another very important role type in Peking opera. Among the many excellent actors and actresses to have specialized in *dan* roles in the history of Peking opera are the famous "Four Great *Dan* Actors"(*Si Da Ming Dan*) - Mei Lanfang, Shang Xiaoyun, Cheng Yanqiu and Xun Huisheng. They made significant contributions to the performance of *dan* roles, enriching Peking opera and helping it develop.

Dan actors play women. *Dan* roles can be divided into such subtypes as *qingyi* (demure type), *huadan* (vivacious young woman), *xiaodan* (young maiden), *wudan* (military woman), *laodan* (elderly woman) and *huashan* (young and beautiful comic woman).

1 Qingyi – Demure Type

Qingyi characters are generally dignified, serious and honest. Most of them are faithful wives, loving mothers or chaste, undefiled women in feudal society. The role type got its name from the characters' black dress (qingyi literally meaning "black dress"). It is also known as zhengdan (chief dan) because of its primary position among all the dan subtypes. The characters are generally young or middle-aged.

Qingyi: a woman from a poor family

Qingyi performances, limited by the personality of the characters, traditionally feature intensive singing and slight, sedate movements. In ancient China, the restrictions of ethical codes and doctrines meant that women did not have freedom of action. They were forbidden from looking sideways, showing their teeth while smiling, or stretching their fingers out of their sleeves. They were required to walk slowly and steadily. In the past, therefore, *qingyi* characters always moved slowly on stage, with one hand resting between their chest and stomach, and the other hand drooping by their side, whether they were sitting or standing. Thus, audiences gave *qingyi* characters the graphic and humorous name of "stomach-holding *dan*" (*baoduzi dan*).

Qingyi: a woman from a rich family

A poster advertising Mei Lanfang's 1935 performance in Moscow

Qingyi characters can also be empresses and imperial concubines. They look sedate and graceful in a *mang* or *gongyi* (imperial dress) and wear a jade belt.

Qingyi: Mei Lanfang as Yang Yuhuan in *The Drunken Beauty* (*Guifei Zuijiu*)

The *qingyi* role includes empresses and imperial concubines

Mang for Women

Women's mang are a bit shorter than those of men and show the long skirt underneath.

Mang for women come in fewer colors than those for men. Yellow mang are exclusive to empresses, red mang are worn by imperial concubines and noblewomen, and yellow-green mang are worn by elderly noblewomen.

Instead of dragons, women's mang usually have a design of red phoenixes flying toward the sun, surrounded by such patterns as a sun, moon, waves and ripples of water.

女白蟒

WORN BY EMPRESS IN MOURNING

The Female White Mang

A woman's *mang* robe

A woman's *mang*. Yang Yuhuan in
The Drunken Beauty (*Guifei Zuijiu*)

Gongyi — Imperial Dresses

Gongyi are dresses derived from women's mang and are usually worn by such female characters as imperial concubines and princesses. They are more brightly colored and luxurious than women's mang.

Women's mang are worn on formal occasions, while gongyi are more casual.

Gongyi: A dress for casual occasions

WORN BY PRINCESSES, GIRLS OF THE NOBILITY, & FAIRIES

宫衣

The Palace Clothing

Huadan: These characters' costumes are generally brightly colored

There have been many outstanding actors playing *qingyi* roles, a very important subtype of *dan*. The four most famous *dan* actors - Mei Lanfang, Shang Xiaoyun, Cheng Yanqiu and Xun Huisheng - all excelled at playing *qingyi* characters.

2 Huadan — Vivacious, Young Women

Huadan characters are young women with a lively, cheerful disposition who move with agility. They are mostly from humble families or are the maidservants of rich families.

The *huadan* costume is unlike that of *qingyi* characters, comprising short blouses and trousers and more brightly colored robes.

Huadan performers dance and speak.

Huadan characters are usually lively.

3 Wudan – Military Women

Wudan characters are women skilled in martial arts, including women generals, heroic forest outlaws, nymphs and fairies.

There are two *wudan* subtypes. One is *duanda wudan* (military women in jackets and trousers), who do not ride a horse. Performers of this subtype speak and perform martial arts.

Wudan characters, also called *daomadan* characters, are skilled in martial arts

The other subtype is *changkao wudan* (armor-clad military woman). This subtype appears in a suit of armor and helmet, generally rides on a horse, and holds a relatively small sword in her hand. This subtype is therefore also known as *daomadan*, meaning "woman who holds a sword and rides on a horse."

A performance of *Women Generals of the Yang Family* (*Yangmen Nüjiang*)

Wudan: The whip she is holding in her right hand indicates that she is riding a horse.

4 Huashan – "Colorful Dress" – Young and Beautiful Comic Women

Huashan roles make up a very important *dan* subtype and were established by Wang Yaoqing. Before the emergence of this subtype, the leading women in plays were traditionally *qingyi* and *huadan*, which are mutually exclusive roles. Audiences found those *dan* characters monotonous, having either too much singing or too much dancing, so performances needed to be extended and enriched to enhance the expressive effect. Seeing this, Wang Yaoqing created a *dan* subtype whose performance embraced singing, speech, acrobatics and dancing, by merging the sedateness of *qingyi* characters, the liveliness of *huadan*, and the martial arts movements and postures of *wudan*. In this way, the range of performance of the *dan* role type was expanded, and the artistic performance in this area was greatly enhanced.

Wang Yaoqing (left) as Sister Yu in *South Gate to Heaven* (*Nantian Men*)

Cheng Yanqiu, Shang Xiaoyun and Mei Lanfang (left to right) performing in *Rainbow Pass* (*Hongni Guan*)

The emergence of *huashan* gradually made the *dan* role type a thriving one, changing the situation whereby *sheng* roles dominated the Peking opera stage. In newly written plays, most of the characters played by the four most famous *dan* actors — Mei Lanfang, Shang Xiaoyun, Cheng Yanqiu and Xun Huisheng — were *huashan* roles.

Mei Lanfang as Hongxian in *Hongxian Steals the Box* (*Hongxian Dao He*)

Xun Huisheng as Li Fengjie in *Meilong Town* (*Meilong Zhen*)

5 Laodan – Elderly Women

Laodan characters are elderly women. When singing and speaking, laodan performers use their real voices, which are rich, loud, high-pitched and melodious.

Laodan characters wear different costumes, such as mang and zhezi (xuezi) robes and pei cloaks, according to their status and the occasion.

Some laodan characters sing most of time, and others mostly act. The distinguished laodan actor Gong Yunfu was able to establish his character through both singing and movement, and greatly contributed to renovating and improving this kind of role.

Laodan: She Saihua in Yang Silang Visits His Mother (Silang Tan Mu)

A laodan character in a zhezi robe

方居
DAN-FEMALE ROLES

6 Caidan – Comic Women

Caidan are also known as *choupozi*. Such characters are cheerful, humorous or shrewish, sly women. *Caidan* characters have traditionally been played by clown (*chou*) actors but are now also sometimes played by *huadan* or *laodan* actors and actresses.

Caidan actors and actresses sing and speak with their real voices, speaking more often than singing. Acting, especially in a farcical way, comprises the bulk of their performance. The actions and makeup of *caidan* characters are exaggerated for comic effect.

Caidan: The character Wan Shi in Song Shijie

Some *dan* characters are women of ethnic minorities, who generally wear a cheongsam (*qipao*).

Wang Yaoqing as Empress Dowager Xiao in *Yanmen Pass* (*Yanmen Guan*). The Manchurian dress she is wearing shows that the character is from an ethnic minority.

Qipao — Cheongsam

Like jianyi *(an archer's attire)*, the qipao or cheongsam was introduced into Peking opera as a new costume in the later years of the Qing Dynasty. It is an embellished version of the real cheongsam.

The cheongsam was a traditional dress worn by Manchurian women and the predecessor of the modern cheongsam. On the Peking opera stage, it is longer and looser. Plays in which the cheongsam can be seen are not necessarily set in the Qing Dynasty because the costume version is not limited by the time period. Female ethnic-minority characters all wear a cheongsam, regardless of the time period.

Mei Lanfang in *Stealing the Token of Authority* (*Dao Ling*), wearing a *qipao* (cheongsam)

Jing — Painted-Face Roles

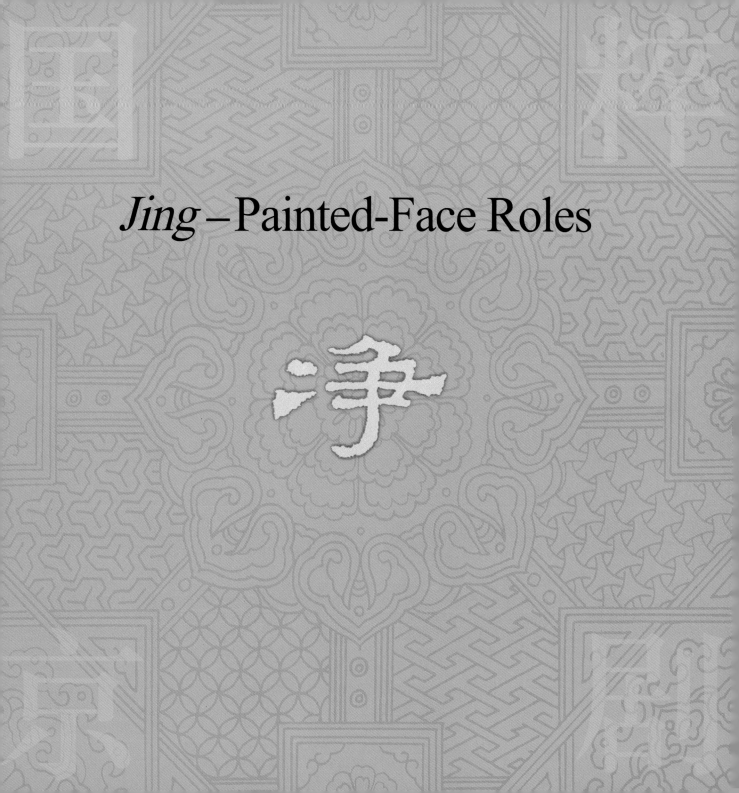

The *jing* is a romantic, exaggerated type of Peking opera role. The characters are mostly cheerful, honest, gallant and intrepid men or treacherous and cruel men.

Jing characters wear colorful paint on their faces, so they are also known as *hualian* or *huamian* (both meaning "painted face").

Jing characters can be divided into *zhengjing* (primary painted-face roles), *fujing* (secondary painted-face roles) and *wujing* (military painted-face roles). There were also *hongjing* (red painted-face roles), which later merged with *hongsheng* (red-faced man roles) and were classed as the *laosheng* (elderly man) role type.

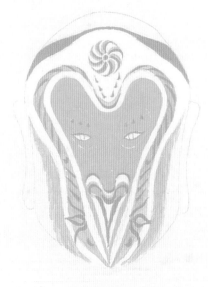

Facial Makeup

Facial makeup in Peking opera is a uniquely Chinese makeup style. Characters from history fall into different categories and have different dispositions. As time went by, such characters were classified and represented by matching types of facial makeup. By portraying the characters' features and lines of the face in an exaggerated way, the facial makeup depicts the character's personality and mental and physical characteristics. There is also facial makeup for immortals and demons, such as the Monkey King and Erlangshen.

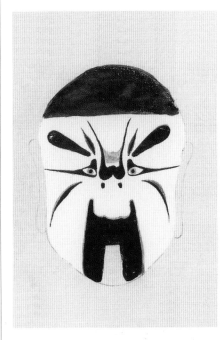
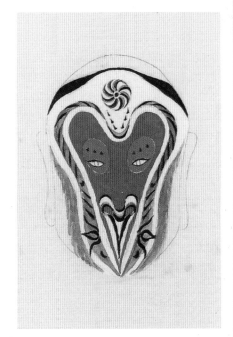

Painted faces

Red face: Jiang Wei in *Iron Cage Mountain* (*Tielong Shan*)

The facial makeup shows the character's personality and type in two ways: color and shape. One major feature of Peking opera is how a character's temperament, personality, role and fate are symbolized by a certain color of face paint. This is also a key to helping the audience understand the plot. For example, a red face represents loyalty and gallantry, while a black face represents an unyielding nature, uprightness, bravery and sometimes rashness. Yellow and white faces are generally used for treacherous ministers and vicious men. Golden and silver faces are used for mysterious immortals and spirits. The different lines drawn on the faces also have different meanings. In short, the colors of the facial makeup show the characters' personalities, while the facial lines indicate the strength of these character traits.

The original functions of facial makeup in Peking opera were to exaggerate the characters' features and facial lines and to express their personalities and mental and physical characteristics in order to strengthen the overall plot of the play. The makeup later became more detailed and was further subdivided until it turned into a decorative art.

Black face, Gao Wang in *Herding Tigers Pass* (*Muhu Guan*) (Performer: Qi Xiaoyun)

The pagoda-holding heavenly king Li Jing, a character in *Wreaking Havoc in Heaven*, is an immortal in the Heavenly Palace.

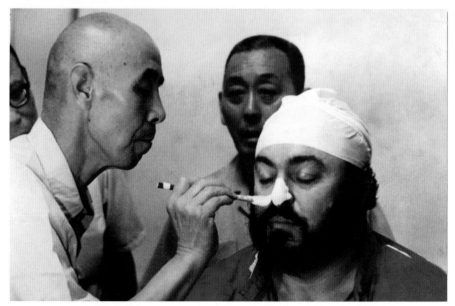

Luciano Pavarotti is very interested in Peking opera. The picture shows a makeup artist painting his face during the Italian singer's visit to Beijing.

1 Zhengjing–Primary Painted- Face Roles

Zhengjing is also known as *damian* ("big face"), *dahuamian* and *dahualian* (both meaning "big painted face").

A *zhengjing* performer mainly sings, so this type of role is also called "singing painted face" (*changgong hualian*).

The singing painted face is also called *tongchui* ("bronze hammer") and *heitou* ("black head").

There is a *hualian* character called Xu Yanzhao in the play *Entering the Palace for the Second Time* (*Er Jin Gong*). He is a typical singing painted-face character, moving very little. As he is always seen holding a bronze hammer in his hand, the hammer became an alias for the singing painted-face role.

Tongchui ("bronze hammer") is a singing painted face — a *changgong hualian* role. (Performer: Qi Xiaoyun)

◀ *Heitou* or black head is also a singing painted face — *a changgong hualian* role. (Performer: Qi Xiaoyun)

Qiu Shengrong as Yao Qi in *General Yao Qi* (*Yao Qi*)

There are many plays about the honest official Lord Bao (Bao Zheng). The character wears black paint on his face and is called "black head."As most part of his performance consists of singing, the term "black head" has also become a synonym for singing painted face.

Most *zhengjing* characters are serious, loyal officials and generals who firmly uphold justice, like the abovementioned Xu Yanzhao and Bao Zheng.

The famous Peking opera performer Qiu Shengrong (1915-71) specialized in *zhengjing* roles. He excelled at expressing the characters' complex thoughts and feelings through exaggerated movements and a solemn bearing.

2 Fujing – Secondary Painted-Face Roles

Fujing characters cover a wide range. Most of them are *jiazi hualian* (painted face of action), called *jiazihua* for short.

Jiazihua actors mainly move about, strike postures, and speak on stage. An excellent *jiazihua* actor is versatile, with a sound grounding in martial arts, skilled at acting, speaking and singing, and with beautiful movements and postures.

In Peking opera, historical characters who are treacherous officials, such as Cao Cao, Dong Zhuo, Jia Sidao and Yan Song, wear no colored paint on their faces but some white powder mixed with glycerol and some black facial lines. This kind of makeup, indicating a bad character, is called "treacherous official face" or" powder face." Such characters are mostly played by *jiazihua* actors.

The famous Peking opera performers Jin Shaoshan, Hao Shouchen and Hou Xirui were excellent at playing *jiazihua* characters. They were renowned as the "Three Most Famous Painted Faces" (*San Da Ming Jing*).

The character Cao Cao in *Yangping Pass* (*Yangping Guan*) (Performer: Qi Xiaoyun)

Jin Shaoshan as Sima Shi in *Forcing the Emperor to Abdicate* (*Hong Bi Gong*)

Hao Shouchen as Yu Chigong in *The Imperial Orchard* (*Yu Guoyuan*)

Hou Xirui as Dou Erdun in *Stealing the Imperial Horse* (*Dao Yu Ma*)

Wujing—Military Painted-Face Roles

Wujing roles are also known as wu'erhua (military secondary painted faces) or shuaida hualian (acrobatic painted faces) because the performers mainly do acrobatic fighting and tumbling and not much singing or speaking. To meet the characters' requirements, wujing actors have to master very difficult martial arts skills.

Wujing characters are mostly brave and tough men. Some are immortals and demons.

Wujing (Performer: Qi Xiaoyun)

Wujing: Cao Hong in *The Long Slope* (*Changban Po*)

Wujing: The character Erlangshen in *The Peach Banquet* (*Pantao Hui*) has a golden painted face, which implies that he is an immortal in the Heavenly Palace.

Chou – Clowns

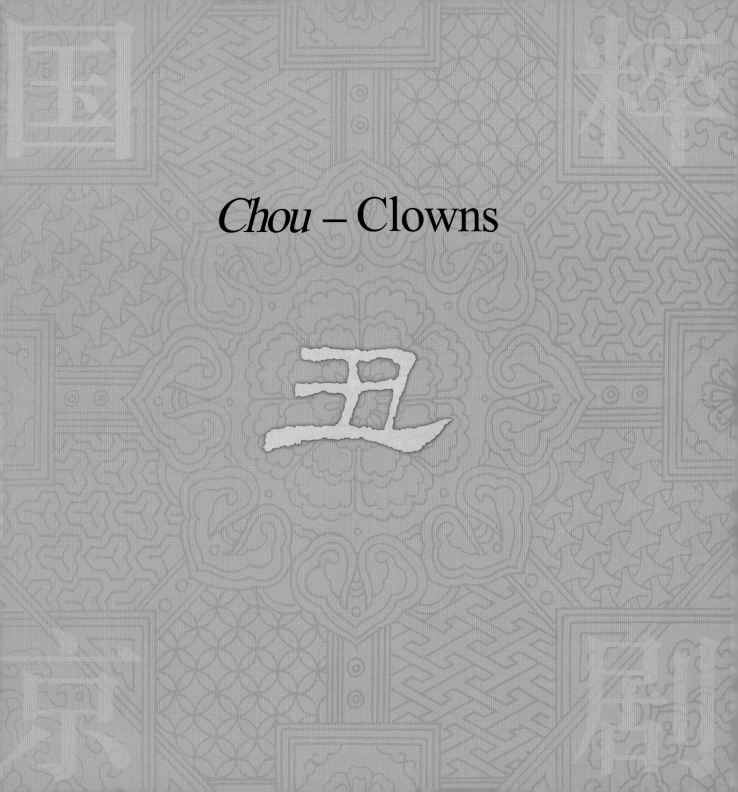

Chou characters are humorous or insidious men.

There are *wenchou* (comic civilian roles) and *wuchou* (acrobatic-fighting comic roles). Performances of the former roles mainly consist of speaking, acting and singing, while those of the latter involve speaking and acrobatic fighting.

The makeup of *chou* characters features a white patch on the bridge of the nose, which can be in any of a variety of shapes, such as a rectangle, ingot or date stone. The size and shape of the patch differ between characters.

Except for the treacherous ones, most *chou* characters are sharp-witted, clever, humorous and even honest and kindhearted. In traditional Peking opera plays, working people of a low social status are mostly *chou* characters. They are often humorous, lively and cheerful. Some are positive characters, such as patriots.

1 Wenchou – Comic Civilian Roles

Wenchou characters wear a white patch on the bridge of the nose, which looks smaller and more delicate than the facial makeup of *jing* characters. Therefore, *wenchou* roles are also known as *xiao hualian* (small painted faces).

Wenchou characters are varied. There are relatively serious characters such as scholars, teachers and officials (usually low-level ones) but more often the characters are working people of low status, such as fishermen, farmers, woodcutters, bartenders, night watchmen, bailiffs and page boys.

Chou character

Chou
character

Wenchou: a witty county magistrate

Wenchou: a bailiff (left) of low social status

The renowned *wenchou* performer Xiao Changhua was popular with audiences for his perfect singing, his clear speaking voice and his vivid performance as the character Chong Gongdao in the play *Escorting the Woman Prisoner* (*Nü Qijie*).

95

2 Wuchou— Acrobatic-Fighting Comic Roles

Wuchou roles are also known as *kaikoutiao* ("talkers and jumpers") because the actor is required not only to be good at jumping but also to speak fluently and clearly.

The *wuchou* roles are mostly heroic men or chivalrous swordsmen, who are exceptionally adept at martial arts skills, agile in movement, humorous and quick-witted.

Ye Shengzhang (1912-66), a renowned *wuchou* actor, was popular with the audiences for his brisk and vigorous movements, clear enunciation and eloquence.

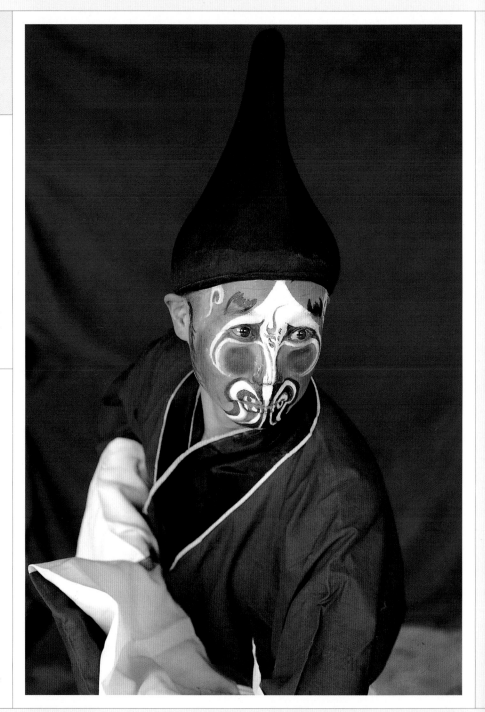

Wuchou: Shi Qian in *Shi Qian Steals a Chicken* (*Shi Qian Tou Ji*)

Ye Shengzhang as Shi Qian in *The Theft of the Armor* (*Dao Jia*)

A production of *Reconciliation of the General and Minister* (*Jiang Xiang He*), with *longtao* actors standing at the back

A *longtao* costume

Longtao Walk-on Parts

Longtao refers to soldiers, hired hands and other members of an entourage.

The term *longtao* literally means dragon-design costume and was originally the name of the costume worn on stage by entourage members and soldiers because such costumes are embroidered with dragon designs. Later it was used to refer to walk-on parts.

Longtao characters usually appear on the stage in groups, each group (*tang*) consisting of four people. To show a large crowd on stage and enhance the atmosphere, usually one or two *longtao* groups are used.

According to plays' different requirements, *longtao* groups come in various sizes and formations. In each formation, the *longtao* actors sing a matching tune. On stage, *longtao* run after the chief commander, bringing changes to the atmosphere and environment, so playing a *longtao* role is also called "running *longtao*." As well as running, *longtao* sometimes stand still at both sides of the stage to bring out the awesome atmosphere in a palace or court.

龍套衣

WORN BY MILITARY ATTENDANTS

The Lung Tao 3

Appendix

附录

I. Main Peking Opera Schools and Their Representative Plays

1 Sheng Roles

"Former Three Schools" of *Laosheng*

Cheng School: Cheng Changgeng (1812-83) was one of the "Three Outstanding Laosheng Actors" (Laosheng "San Jie"). His representative plays included Meeting of Heroes (Qunying Hui).

Yu School: Yu Sansheng was born at the end of the 18th century and died in the mid-19th century. He was another of the "Three Outstanding Laosheng Actors." His representative plays included Ruse of the Empty City (Kongcheng Ji).

Zhang School: Zhang Erkui (1814-60) was one of the "Three Outstanding Laosheng Actors." His representative plays included Beating the Princess (Da Jinzhi).

Cheng Changgeng

"Latter Three Schools" of *Laosheng*

Tan School: Tan Xinpei (1847-1917), a pupil of Cheng Changgeng, specialized in laosheng and was reputed as the "King of Opera Actors." His representative plays included Dingjun Mountain (Dingjun Shan) *and* Yangping Pass (Yangping Guan).

Tan Xinpei

Wang School: Wang Guifen (1860-1909) specialized in laosheng. *His representative plays included* Wenzhao Pass (Wenzhao Guan).

Wang Guifen

Sun Juxian

Sun School: Sun Juxian (1841-1931) spe-cialized in laosheng. *His representative plays included* Dressing Down Yang Guang (Ma Yang Guang).

"Four Great Bearded Men"
(Si Da Xusheng)

Yu School: Yu Shuyan (1890-1943) was a disciple of the Tan School. His representative plays included The Taiping War (Zhan Taiping).

Yu Shuyan (right) as Yue Fei in *Conquering Tanzhou (Zhen Tanzhou)*

Yan Jupeng

Yan School: Yan Jupeng (1889-1942). His representative plays included Beat the Drum to Curse Cao (Ji Gu Ma Cao).

Gao School: Gao Qingkui (1890-1942).
His representative plays included Xiaoyao Ford
(Xiaoyao Jin).

Gao Qingkui as Song Jiang (right) in *The
Black Dragon Courtyard* (*Wulong Yuan*)

Ma Lianliang as Wang Yanling in *Qin Xianglian*

Ma School: Ma Lianliang (1901-66). His representative plays included At the Sweet Dew Temple (Ganlu Si).

Qi School: Zhou Xinfang (1894-1975) specialized in laosheng. *His representative plays included* Eternal Regret of the Last Ming Emperor (Ming Mo Yi Hen).

Zhou Xinfang as Xu Ce in *Xu Ce Running Through the Town*(*Xu Ce Pao Cheng*)

Yang Baosen as Huang Zhong in *Dingjun Mountain* (*Dingjun Shan*)

Yang School: Yang Baosen (1909-85) spe-cialized in laosheng. *His representative plays included* Beat the Drum to Curse Cao (Ji Gu Ma Cao).

Xi School: Xi Xiaobo (1910-77) special-ized in laosheng. *His representative plays in-cluded* Joint Company Barracks (Lianying Zhai).

Wusheang

Yang School: Yang Xiaolou (1877-1938). His representative plays included The Long Slope (Changban Po).

Yang Xiaolou

Gai School: Gai Jiaotian (1888-1971). His representative plays included Where Three Roads Meet (San Cha Kou).

Gai Jiaotian

Xiaosheng

Ye School: Ye Shenglan (1915-79). His representative plays included Meeting of Heroes (Qunying Hui).

Ye Shenglan as Luo Cheng in *Luo Cheng*

2 *Dan*

Wang School: Wang Yaoqing (1882-1954) specialized in qingyi *roles. He founded the* huashan *role type by combining some features of* qingyi *and* huadan *roles and had a great influence on later* dan *actors. His representative plays included* Yanmen Pass (Yanmen Guan).

Wang Yaoqing

"The Four Great *Dan* Actors"

Mei School: Mei Lanfang (1894-1961). In the early years of his career, he mainly played qingyi *characters. Later he learned how to play* huadan *and* daomadan *characters and, using his* huadan *and* daomadan *skills, broke with the traditional* qingyi *performance of singing with little expression or movement. He also made bold innovations in the characters' makeup, hair decorations and costumes, and invented many new dance movements, enriching the performance of Peking opera. His representative plays included* The Drunken Beauty (Guifei Zui Jiu), Farewell, My Concubine (Bawang Bie Ji) *and* Mu Guiying Takes Command (Mu Guiying Guashuai).

Shang School: Shang Xiaoyun (1899-1976). The Shang School created a group of heroines. His representative plays included Liang Hongyu.

Cheng School: Cheng Yanqiu (1904-58) was famous for performing in tragedies. His representative plays included Tears on a Barren Mountain (Huang Shan Lei).

Xun School: Of the four great dan *actors, Xun Huisheng (1899-1968) wrote and played in the most new plays. His representative plays included* Courtesan Yu Tangchun (Yu Tangchun) *and* The Red Maid (Hong Niang).

The four great *dan* actors: (left to right) Cheng Yanqiu, Shang Xiaoyun, Mei Lanfang and Xun Huisheng

Gong School: Gong Yunfu (1862-1932) specialized in laodan *roles. His representative plays included* Xu's Mother Reviles Cao Cao (Xu Mu Ma Cao).

Gong Yunfu as She Saihua in *Lady She Takes Her Leave of the Imperial Court* (*Taijun Ci Chao*)

Li School: Li Duokui (1898-1974) specialized in laodan *roles. His repesentative plays included* Watching-for-the-Son Tower (Wang Er Lou).

3 *Jing*

Jin School: Jin Shaoshan (1889-1945), one of the "three great *jing* actors," was good at playing Lord Bao. His representative plays included *The Execution of Chen Shimei* (*Zha Mei An*) and *Entering the Palace for the Second Time* (*Er Jin Gong*).

Jin Shaoshan

Hao Shouchen

Hou Xirui

Hao School: Hao Shouchen (1887-1961), one of the "three great *jing* actors," specialized in *fujing* (*jiazi hualian*) roles. His representative plays included *Linked-Strategy Fortress* (*Lianhuantao*).

Hou School: Hou Xirui *(1892-1983)*, one of the "three great *jing* actors," specialized in *fujing* (*jiazi hualian*) roles. His representative plays included *The Battle of Wancheng* (*Zhan Wancheng*) and *Stealing the Imperial Horse*

(*Dao Yu Ma*).

Qiu School: Qiu Shengrong (1915-71) specialized in *zhengjing* roles. His representative plays included *General Yao Qi* (*Yao Qi*) and *The Execution of Chen Shimei* (*Zha Mei An*).

Yuan School: Yuan Shihai (1916-2002) was a disciple of the Hao School. His representative plays included *Stealing the Imperial Horse* (*Dao Yu Ma*).

Qiu Shengrong as Gao Wang in *Tending Tigers Pass(Muhu Guan)*

Yuan Shihai as Zhang Dingbian in *At the Mouth of the Jiujiang River* (*Jiujiang Kou*)

4 *Chou*

Liu Gansan (1817-94) was a representative *chou* actor during Peking opera's initial years. He was good at playing *wenchou* characters. His representative plays included *Visiting the In-Laws (Tan Qingjia).*

Wang Changlin as Yang Xiangwu in *Three Attempts to Steal the Nine-Dragon Cup (San Dao Jiulongbei)*

Xiao Changhua as Chong Gongdao in *Escorting the Woman Prisoner* (*Nü Qijie*)

Wang Changlin (1858-1931) specialized in *wuchou* roles and sometimes played *wenchou* characters. His representative plays included *Shi Qian Steals a Chicken* (*Shi Qian Tou Ji*). His disciple Fu Xiaoshan was also an excellent *wuchou* actor.

Xiao Changhua (1878-1967) specialized in *wenchou* roles. He worked with many famous Peking opera actors. In 1922, he began a long-term collaboration with Mei Lanfang. His representative plays included *Escorting the Woman Prisoner* (*Nü Qijie*). He was also a famous Peking opera educator, having trained many highly talented people.

Modern Peking Opera

Modern Peking opera mainly refers to those operas that reflect life since the 1950s. In the 1960s and 1970s, in particular, plays reached a high standard of writing and performance, making Peking opera influential and known to every household in China. Representative modern operas include *Shajia Creek* (*Shajia Bang*) and *Taking Tiger Mountain by Strategy* (*Zhi Qu Weihu Shan*).

A production of the modern Peking opera play *Shajia Creek* (*Shajia Bang*)

II. Main Musical Instruments of Peking Opera

1 Wind Instruments

Bamboo flute (*di*)

The bamboo flute is played horizontally, in solos, ensembles or as accompaniment.

Sheng

A reed pipe instrument mainly used as accompaniment or in ensembles or solos.

***Suona* horn**

A woodwind instrument that makes a sharp, clear sound, usually used as accompaniment or in solos to enhance the atmosphere of grand occasions such as the launching of attacks, feasts and celebrations.

A *suona* horn

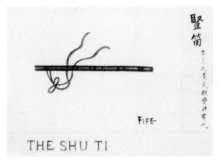

THE SHU TI — FIFE

A flute (*di*)

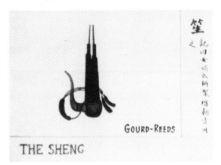

THE SHENG — GOURD-REEDS

A *sheng*

2 Stringed Instruments

Sanxian

A three-stringed plucked instrument. Large sanxian are popular in northern China and small sanxian in the south. The instrument is mainly used as accompaniment.

Pipa

A plucked stringed instrument played by holding it vertically with one hand and plucking the strings with the five fingers of the other. It is used in solos, as accompaniment and in ensembles.

A *pipa*

THE SAN HSIEN — 3. STRING BANJO

A *sanxian*

THE P'I PA — MANDOLIN

Huqin

A category of bowed instruments.

Erhu

A bowed instrument. A kind of *huqin*, it makes a low, soft, expressive sound. It makes solemn and stirring tunes especially moving.

Jinghu

A bowed instrument. A kind of *huqin*, it makes a vigorous, resonant sound, usually used as accompaniment in Peking opera.

Yueqin

A plucked stringed instrument that makes a clear sound and is used in solos, as accompaniment and in ensembles.

3 Percussion Instruments

Danpi drum (*danpi gu*)

An instrument used in percussion and orchestral music to keep time for the other instruments, beating out the tempo together with the ban when the actor or actress is singing. The player is called the *gushi* (drum master).

Ban (clappers)

Mainly used to beat out the tempo during singing or to keep time for the other instruments, together with the *danpi* drum.

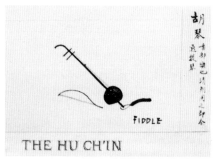

THE HU CH'IN

A *huqin*

THE HU CH'IN

An *erhu* — two-stringed fiddle

THE TAN P'I KU

A *danpi* drum

THE HU CH'IN

A *jinghu* or Peking opera fiddle

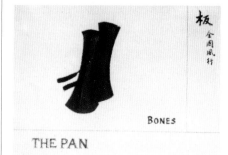

THE YUEH CH'IN

A *yueqin* or Chinese mandolin

THE PAN

Bamboo clappers (*ban*)

They are played by the *gushi* (drum master).

Tanggu drum

Used in such scenes as wars, the calling of meetings of generals, the convening of courts, and executions, or played alongside the *suona* horn.

Gong (*luo*)

There are bigger and smaller gongs. In Peking opera, the bigger gong is also called the *jing* gong (*jingluo*). It makes a loud and sonorous sound and is mostly used when generals enter or leave the stage and in battle scenes. The smaller gong gives a clear, re-sounding sound and is often played when scholars, women or comic characters enter or leave the stage or to accompany the charac-ters' various minor movements.

Cymbals (*bo*)

The cymbals consist of two metal plates that produce a sound when struck against each other. They accompany the big or small gong, strengthening the tempo and acting as a link between beats. Larger cymbals are called *nao* or *naobo*.

Big *nao*

Also called big *bo* (cymbals), these con-sist of two parts that make a loud and power-ful sound when struck against each other. They are used to enhance the atmosphere or sym-bolize the sound of the wind and waves.

A *tanggu* drum

A gong (*luo*)

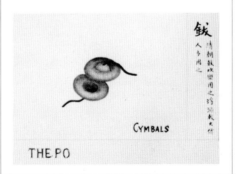

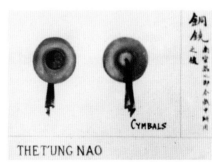

Cymbals

Big *nao* cymbals

III. Main Props in Peking Opera

Broadsword (*dao*)

Spear (*qiang*)

Sword (*jian*)

Halberd (*ji*)

War hammer (*chui*)

Battle-ax (*fu*)

Shield (*dun*)

Banner (*dao*)

General's banner (*shuaiqi*)

Arrows to accompany orders (*lingjian*)

Whip to represent a horse (*mabian*)

Fan

Staff (*guaizhang*)

Lantern

Arrows to accompany commands

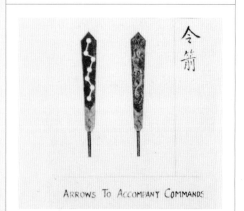

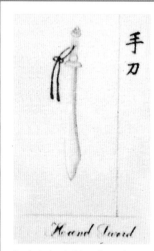

A single-handed broadsword

A long-handled broadsword

A spear

A sword (*jian*)

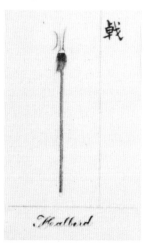

A halberd (*ji*)

A war hammer (*chui*)

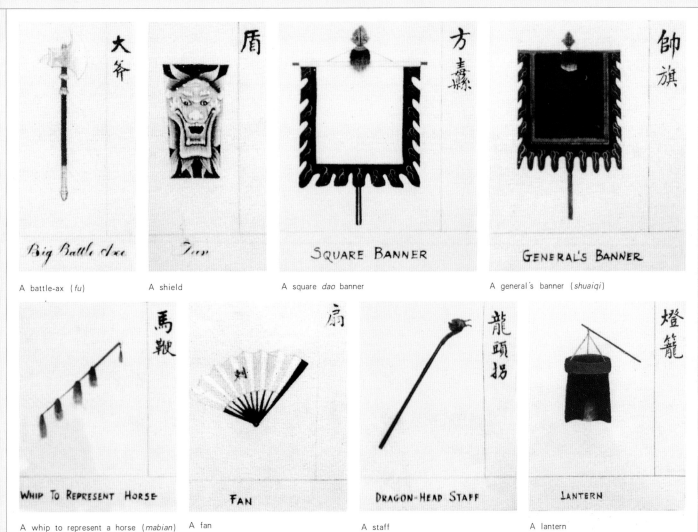

大斧
Big Battle Axe

A battle-ax (*fu*)

盾
Fan

A shield

方壽縣
SQUARE BANNER

A square *dao* banner

帥旗
GENERAL'S BANNER

A general's banner (*shuaiqi*)

馬鞭
WHIP TO REPRESENT HORSE

A whip to represent a horse (*mabian*)

扇
FAN

A fan

龍頭拐
DRAGON-HEAD STAFF

A staff

燈籠
LANTERN

A lantern

黑大纛
LARGE BANNER

A large black *dao* banner

IV. Types of Facial Makeup in Peking Opera

Full-facial makeup (*zheng lian*)

One color of paint is applied to the whole face to exaggerate the face's skin color, and the character's expression is shown by highlighting his brows, eyes, nose and mouth and by drawing the fine lines of his facial muscles.

Three-part, or "three-tile," face(*sankuaiwa lian*)

This is based on the full-facial makeup but the brows, eyes and nose are further ex aggerated by lines drawn around the eyes and nose, hence the name of this kind of makeup. The three-part face can vary a lot to show different characters, including both positive ones such as loyal and brave people and negative ones such as local tyrants and bullies.

Cross-marked face (*shizimen lian*)

Having developed from the three-part face, this features a cross shape formed by the main facial color, which is reduced to a vertical strip and makeup around the eyes. This is a face of positive characters such as heroes and generals.

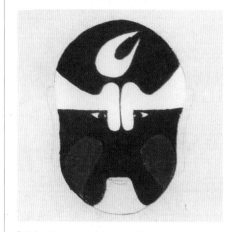
Full-facial makeup (*zheng lian*)

Full-facial makeup

Three-part (three-tile) face (*sankuaiwa lian*)

Cross-marked face (*shizimen lian*)

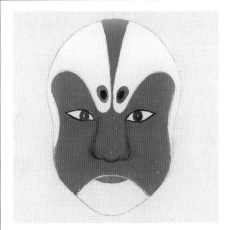

Sixty-percent or six-tenths face (*liufen lian*)

Multi-patterned fragmentary face (*suihua lian*)

Twisted face (*wai lian*)

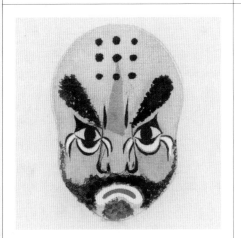

Buddhist and Taoist monk's face (*seng-dao lian*)

Eunuch's face (*taijian lian*)

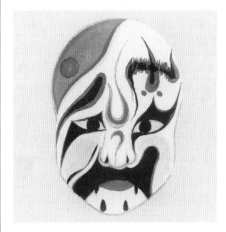

Ingot-pattern face (*yuanbao lian*)

Sixty-percent face or six-tenths face (*liufen lian*)

Having developed from the full-facial makeup, this features a reduced forehead color and exaggerated brows. The white brows take up 40 percent of the whole face, while the main facial color takes up 60 percent, hence the name of the makeup. It is also called "elderly man's face" (*lao lian*). Characters wearing such makeup are white-haired and white-bearded, loyal senior generals.

Multi-patterned fragmented face (*suihua lian*)

Developed from the three-part face, this features varied colors and patterns, and fine broken lines in a complicated pattern. Characters wearing such makeup are mostly intrepid generals and forest outlaws.

Twisted face (*wai lian*)

The facial lines are asymmetrical to produce a twisted effect. Characters wearing such makeup are mostly ugly and negative ones with twisted features but, in some cases, they are special positive characters.

Buddhist and Taoist monks' faces (*seng-dao lian*)

This is the makeup of characters who are Buddhist or Taoist monks. The Buddhist monk's face is similar to the three-part face in composition. The Taoist monk's face is basically the three-part face but with the two brow areas joined.

Eunuch's face (*taijian lian*)

This is the makeup of eunuchs who usurped power and persecuted people. It is in red and white, with a composition similar to that of the full-facial makeup and three-part face.

Ingot-pattern face (*yuanbao lian*)

The forehead color is different from the rest of the face and is in the shape of an ingot, hence the name of the makeup. Both positive and negative characters may wear this makeup.

Symbolic pictographic face (*xiangxing lian*)

This represents such characters as spirits, immortals and demons in fairy-tale operas.

Symbolic pictographic face (*xiangxing lian*)

Immortal's face (*shenxian lian*)

Immortal's face (*shenxian lian*)

Golden and silver colors are applied to show the sacredness and solemnity of such characters as immortals and Buddha.

Clown face (*choujue lian*)

Also known as smaller painted face (*xiao hualian*), this makeup features a white patch in the center over the bridge of the nose. The character's comic characteristics are shown in an exaggerated way. Clown faces represent a wide range of characters, from emperors, civilian and military officials, down to banner-bearers, muleteers, parasol carriers and scouts, including both positive and negative characters.

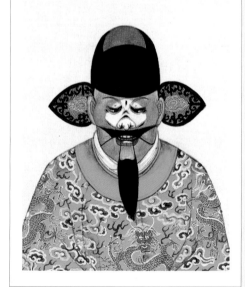

Clown face (*choujue lian*)

V. Peking Opera Theaters

Qing Dynasty imperial theaters

Beijing's imperial theaters were large in scale. The most famous ones included the theater by Nanhai Lake, the one in the Garden of Abundant Water (Fengze Yuan), the one in the Palace of Eternal Spring (Changchun Gong), the theater in the Study of Pure Fragrance (Shufang Zhai), and the Grand Theater in the Summer Palace.

The Summer Palace's towering Grand Theater has a complicated structure and ingenious design. It was specially built for the 60th birthday of Empress Dowager Cixi. It took three years and a huge amount of funds to build.

Pavilion of Cheerful Melodies (*Changyin Ge*), a theater at the Palace of Peace and Longevity (*Ningshou Gong*) in the Forbidden City

The "Reserved Refinement" (*Fengya Cun*) indoor opera stage in the Forbidden City's Study of Pure Fragrance (*Shufang Zhai*)

The Summer Palace's Grand Theater

Painting of an imperial theater

Copies of Forbidden City imperial plays

Folk stages

During New Year holidays, festivals, harvest time and celebrations, stages are built for performances at a village entrance or by the road. Such stages are usually simple and are removed after the celebration.

Home theaters

In the past, on occasions to celebrate, rich families would hire Peking opera actors and actresses to perform at their homes, where there would be a permanent or temporary stage.

Amateur gatherings

Many Peking opera enthusiasts gather in a street or lane or in a corner of a park and entertain themselves by singing Peking opera arias.

A rural opera stage from the Qing Dynasty

Rural opera stage from the Qing Dynasty

Rural opera stage from the Qing Dynasty

Peking opera show at the Guanghe Teahouse during
Qing Emperor Jiaqing's reign (1796—1820)

Modern theater

Modern theater

The interior of Beijing's Chang'an Theater

The audience watches a performance in a modern theater.

A mansion's home theater in the late Qing Dynasty

143

Amateurs sing at the Temple of Heaven

A production of *The Phoenix Returns to Its Nest* (*Feng Huan Chao*) performed by a University of Hawaii troupe from the United States

VI. Glossary of Chinese Terms

Baishe Zhuan 《白蛇传》 the opera *Tale of the White Snake*

Baishui Tan 《白水滩》 the opera *White-Water Beach*

ban 板 bamboo clappers (percussion instrument)

banshi 板式 type of meter for Peking opera music

baoduzi dan 抱肚子旦 "stomach-holding *dan*," a humorous name for *qingyi* characters

baoyi, baoku 抱衣，抱裤 *bao* jackets and trousers are tight-fitting and worn by chivalrous swordsmen, upright men and heroic forest outlaws

Bawang Bie Ji 《霸王别姬》 the opera *Farewell, My Concubine*

bo 钹 cymbals

buzi 补子 patch worn on the front and back of an official's *guanyi* gown, indicating civilian or military rank

caidan 彩旦 comic woman, female clown

Changban Po 《长坂坡》 the opera *The Long Slope*

changgong hualian 唱工花脸 "singing painted face," another name for *zhengjing*

changkao wudan 长靠武旦 armor-clad female warrior role

changkao wusheng 长靠武生 armor-clad male warrior role

changmian 场面 Peking opera orchestra (literally, "facing the stage")

changqiang 唱腔 Peking opera vocal music

chayi 茶衣 "tea clothes," a short blue cotton *zhezi* (*xuezi*) robe worn by characters of low social status

chou 丑 clown, comic role

choujue lian 丑角脸 clown face, a design of facial makeup used for a wide range of characters

choupozi 丑婆子 another name for *caidan*

chui 锤 war hammer

Chun Qiu Pei 《春秋配》 the opera *The Match of Spring and Autumn*

da hualian 大花脸, da huamian 大花面 "big painted face," alternative terms for *zhengjing*

Da Jinzhi 《打金枝》 the opera *Beating the Princess*

Da Jinzhuan 《打金砖》 the opera *Beating Golden Bricks*

damian 大面 "big face," another name for *zhengjing*

dan 旦 female role

Danao Tiangong 《大闹天宫》 the opera *Wreaking Havoc in Heaven*

danpigu 单皮鼓 *danpi* drum, used to keep time for the other instruments

Dao Jia 《盗甲》 the opera *The Theft of the Armor*

Dao Ling 《盗令》 the opera *Stealing the Token of Authority*

Dao Yu Ma 《盗御马》 the opera *Stealing the Imperial Horse*

dao 刀 broadsword

dao 纛 big army banner

daoma dan 刀马旦 "woman who holds a sword and rides a horse," another name for *changkao wudan*

di 笛 bamboo flute

Dingjun Shan 《定军山》 the opera *Dingjun Mountain*

duanda wudan 短打武旦 role of a female warrior dressed in jacket and trousers

duanda wusheng 短打武生 role of a male warrior dressed in jacket and trousers

dun 盾 shield

Ehu Cun 《恶虎村》 the opera *Ferocious Tiger Village*

Er Jin Gong 《二进宫》 the opera *Entering the Palace for the Second Time*, also known as *The Two Faithful Courtiers*

erhu 二胡 two-stringed fiddle, slightly loner in tone than the *jinghu*

erhuang 二黄 one of the main types of melody in Chinese opera

Fen lian 粉脸 "powder face," the makeup of a historic treacherous official character, usually played by a *jiazihua* actor

Feng Huan Chao 《凤还巢》 the opera *The Phoenix Returns to Its Nest*

fu 斧 battle-ax

fuguiyi 富贵衣 "robe of fortune," basically a zhezi (xuezi) with many small silk patches

fujing 副净 secondary painted-face role with skillful movements

Gan Ning Baiqi Jie Weiying 《甘宁百骑劫魏营》 the opera *Gan Ning Raids the Wei Camp with a Hundred Cavalrymen*

Ganlu Si 《甘露寺》 the opera *At the Sweet Dew Temple*

gongyi 宫衣 imperial dress

gu 鼓 drum

guaizhang 拐杖 staff, a prop used in Peking opera

guanyi 官衣 formal style of gown worn by an official

Guifei Zuijiu 《贵妃醉酒》 the opera *The Drunken Beauty*

gushi 鼓师 drum master, the musician who keeps time for the band using the *danpi* drum and *ban* (clappers)

hangdang 行当 term for role types in Peking opera

heitou 黑头 "black head," a *changgong hualian* role

Hong Bi Gong 《红逼宫》 the opera *Forcing the Emperor to Abdicate*

Hong Niang 《红娘》 the opera *The Red Maid*

hongjing 红净 a former name for *hongsheng* when this role was played by actors specializing in *jing* roles

Hongni Guan 《虹霓关》 the opera *Rainbow Pass*

hongsheng 红生 role of a red-faced young man

Hongxian Dao He 《红线盗盒》 the opera *Hongxian Steals the Box*

huadan 花旦 vivacious young woman, a type of *dan* role

hualian 花脸 "painted face," a *jing* character with a dark-colored painted face

huamian 花面 "painted face," another term for the *jing* role

huangpei 皇帔 "imperial cape," a yellow *pei* cape worn exclusively by emperors and empresses in Peking opera

Huangshan Lei 《荒山泪》 the opera *Tears on a Barren Mountain*

Huarong Dao 《华容道》 the opera *Huarong Pass*

huashan 花衫 young and beautiful comic woman, a type of *dan* role

huqin 胡琴 a category of two-stringed bowedinstrument that includes the *erhu* and *jinghu*

Ji Gu Ma Cao 《击鼓骂曹》 the opera *Beat the Drum to Curse Cao*

jian 剑 sword

jianchen lian 奸臣脸 another term for *fenlian* makeup

Jiang Xiang He 《将相和》 the opera *Reconciliation of the General and Minister*

jianyi wusheng 箭衣武生 archer role

jianyi 箭衣 an archer's clothing

jiazihua 架子花, jiazi hualian 架子花脸 "painted face of action," a kind of *fujing* character who moves about a lot

Jie Dongfeng 《借东风》 the opera *Borrowing the East Wind*

jing 净 painted-face role

jinghu 京胡 two-stringed Peking opera fiddle, slightly higher in tone than the *erhu*

jingju 京剧 Peking opera

jingluo 京锣 the larger gong used in Peking opera

Jiujiang Kou 《九江口》 the opera *At the Mouth of the Jiujiang River*

juchang 剧场, juyuan 剧院 modern European-style theater building

kaichang 开氅 a casual overcoat worn by generals

kaikoutiao 开口跳 "talker and jumper," another name for *wuchou*

kao 靠 military officer's armor

kaoba wusheng 靠把武生, **kao wusheng** 靠武生 armor-clad warrior role

Kongcheng Ji 《空城计》 the opera *Ruse of the Empty City*

Kuaiyi, kuaiku 快衣, 快裤 *kuai* jackets have lines of densely arranged Chinese-style buttons along the underside of the sleeves and the center at the front, while the trousers are black

Kunqu 昆曲 a type of opera based on Kunqiang (昆腔) melodies, popular in southern Jiangsu, Beijing and Hebei

laodan 老旦 elderly woman role

laolian 老脸 elderly man's face, another name for *liufen lian*

laosheng "san jie" 老生"三杰" the three outstanding *laosheng* actors — Cheng Changgeng, Yu Sansheng and Zhang Erkui (程长庚、余三胜、张二奎),whose Cheng School, Yu School and Zhang School make up the "Three Former Schools" of Laosheng (老生"前三派" *laosheng* "*qian san pai*")

laosheng 老生 role of an elderly or middle-aged gentleman

Liang Hongyu 《梁红玉》 the opera *Liang Hongyu*, named after its heroine

Lianhuantao 《连环套》 the opera *Linked Strategy Fortress*

Lianying Zhai 《连营寨》 the opera *Joint Company Barracks*

lingjian 令箭 arrows to accompany orders

liufen lian 六分脸 sixty-percent face or six-tenths face, a design of facial makeup used for senior generals

longtao 龙套 walk-on parts such as soldiers, hired hands and members of an entourage in traditional Chinese opera; literally "dragon-design costume" after the clothes worn by such characters

Luhua He 《芦花河》 the opera *Reed Catkins River*

Luo Cheng 《罗成》 the opera *Luo Cheng*, named after the hero

luo 锣 gong

lüshi 律诗 classical poem of eight lines, each containing five or seven characters, with a strict tonal pattern and rhyme scheme

Ma Yang Guang 《骂杨广》 the opera *Dressing Down Yang Guang*

mabian 马鞭 whip to represent a horse, a prop used in Peking opera

magua 马褂 mandarin jacket, a Qing Dynasty jacket that may be worn by characters of all dynasties in Peking opera

mang 蟒 python-design robe

Ma Shang Yuan 《马上缘》 the opera *Marriage Predestined on Horseback*

Meilong Zhen 《梅龙镇》 the opera *Meilong Town*

Ming Mo Yi Hen 《明末遗恨》 the opera *Eternal Regret of the Last Ming Emperor*

minjian xilou 民间戏楼 folk theater building

Mu Guiying Guashuai 《穆桂英挂帅》 the opera *Mu Guiying Takes Command*

Mudan Ting 《牡丹亭》 the opera *The Peony Pavilion*

Muhu Guan 《牧虎关》 the opera *Tending Tigers Pass*

Nantian Men 《南天门》 the opera *South Gate to Heaven*

nao 铙 a kind of large cymbal

Nü Qijie 《女起解》 the opera *Escorting the Woman Prisoner*, also known as *Courtesan Su San Escorted to Trial* (《苏三起解》 *Su San Qijie*)

Pantao Hui 《蟠桃会》 the opera *The Peach Banquet*

pei 帔 short embroidered cape

pihuang 皮黄 *xipi* and *erhuang*, the two main types of melody in Chinese opera

pipa 琵琶 four-stringed plucked instrument with a fretted fingerboard; also called balloon guitar

Qi Shuang Hui 《奇双会》 the opera *Unexpected Reunion*

Qin Xianglian 《秦香莲》 the opera *Qin Xianglian*, named after its heroine

Qingshi Shan 《青石山》 the opera *The Blue Stone Mountain*

qingyi 青衣 demure woman, a type of *dan* role (literally called "black dress" after the characters' clothing)

qiongsheng 穷生 role of an unfortunate, impoverished scholar, a kind of *xiaosheng* role

qipao 旗袍 cheongsam, a close-fitting woman's dress with a high neck and slit skirt

Qunying Hui 《群英会》 the opera *Meeting of Heroes*

San Cha Kou 《三岔口》 the opera *Where Three Roads Meet*

San Da Ming Jing 三大名净 Peking opera's three great *jing* actors Hao Shouchen, Hou Xirui and Jin Shaoshan (郝寿臣、侯喜瑞、金少山)

San Dao Jiulongbei 《三盗九龙杯》 the opera *Three Attempts to Steal the Nine-Dragon Cup*

Sankuaiwa lian 三块瓦脸 three-part or "three-tile" face, a design of facial makeup

sanxian 三弦 three-stringed plucked instrument

seng-daolian 僧道脸 Buddhist and Taoist monks' faces, a design of facial makeup similar to *sankuaiwa lian*

Shajia Bang 《沙家浜》 the modern opera *Shajia Creek*

Shen Tou Ci Tang 《审头刺汤》 the opera *From Trial of the Severed Head to the Killing of Tang Qin*

sheng 生 male role

sheng 笙 reed pipe (wind instrument)

shenxianlian 神仙脸 immortal's face, a design of facial makeup

Shi Qian Tou Ji 《时迁偷鸡》 the opera *Shi Qian Steals a Chicken*

shizimen lian 十字门脸 cross-marked face, a design of facial makeup used for positive characters such as heroes and generals

shuaida hualian 摔打花脸 "acrobatic painted face," another name for *wujing*

Shuaiqi 帅旗 general's banner

Shui Yan Qi Jun 《水淹七军》 the opera *Guan Yu Floods Seven Armies*

Si Da Ming Dan 四大名旦 Peking opera's four great *dan* actors Mei Lanfang, Shang Xiaoyun, Cheng Yanqiu and Xun Huisheng (梅兰芳、尚小云、程砚秋、荀慧生)

Si Da Xusheng 四大须生 Peking opera's four great bearded-man actors Yu Shuyan, Ma Lianliang, Yan Jupeng and Gao Qingkui (余叔岩、马连良、言菊朋、高庆奎)

Si Jinshi 《四进士》 the opera *Four Newly Appointed Officials*

Silang Tan Mu 《四郎探母》 the opera *Yang Silang Visits His Mother*

Song Shijie 《宋士杰》 the opera *Song Shijie*

Su San Qijie — See *Nü qijie*

suihua lian 碎花脸 multi-patterned fragmented face, a design of facial makeup used mostly for intrepid generals and forest outlaws

suona 唢呐 horn (woodwind instrument)

taijian lian 太监脸 eunuch's face, a design of facial makeup

Taijun Ci Chao 《太君辞朝》 the opera *Lady She Takes Her Leave of the Imperial Court*

Tan Qingjia 《探亲家》 the opera *Visiting the In-Laws*

tang 堂 group (of four *longtao* actors)

tanggu 堂鼓 a kind of drum, used in opera scenes such as wars, the calling of meetings of generals, the convening of courts, and executions

Tielong Shan 《铁笼山》 the opera *Iron Cage Mountain*

tongchui 铜锤 "bronze hammer," another name for *changgong hualian*

wailian 歪脸 twisted face, a design of facial makeup used mostly for negative characters

Wang Er Lou 《望儿楼》 the opera *Watching-for-the-Son Tower*

wawasheng 娃娃生 baby *sheng*, boy role

Wen Qiao Nao Fu 《问樵闹府》 the opera *Asking the Woodsman*

wenchang 文场 orchestra of stringed and wind instruments for

wenxi shows (literally, "civilian stage")

wenchou 文丑 comic civilian role

wenxi 文戏 "gentle show," operatic show focusing on singing and acting rather than acrobatic fighting

Wenzhao Guan 《文昭关》 the oper *Wenzhao Pass*

Wu Song Da Hu 《武松打虎》 the opera *Wu Song Fights a Tiger*

wu'erhua 武二花 "military secondary painted face," another name for *wujing*

wuchang 武场 orchestra of percussion instruments for *wuxi* shows (literally, "military stage")

wuchou 武丑 military or acrobatic-fighting clown role

wudan 武旦 female warrior role

wujing 武净 military painted-face role

Wulong Yuan 《乌龙院》 the opera *The Black Dragon Courtyard*

wusheng 武生 male warrior role

wuxi 武戏 operatic show with a lot of acrobatic fighting

xiangxing lian 象形脸 symbolic pictographic face, a design of facial makeup used for characters such as spirits, immortals and demons

xiao dan 小旦 young maiden, a type of *dan* role

xiao hualian 小花脸 "small painted face," another name for the *wenchou* role; also another name for *choujue lian* design of makeup

xiaosheng 小生 young man role

Xiaoyao Jin 《逍遥津》 the opera *Xiaoyao Ford*

xieyi 写意 painting style using freehand brushwork and aimed at catching the spirit of the subject and expressing the author's mood

xilou 戏楼 theater building

xipi 西皮 one of the main types of melody in Chinese opera

xitai 戏台 stage

Xixiang Ji 《西厢记》 the opera *Romance of the Western Chamber*

Xu the Town

Xu Mu Ma Cao 《徐母骂曹》 the opera *Xu's Mother Reviles Cao Cao*

xusheng 须生 "bearded man," another term for *laosheng*

Yangmen Nü jiang 《杨门女将》 the opera *Women Generals of the Yang Family*

Yangping Guan 《阳平关》 the opera *Yangping Pass*

Yanmen Guan 《雁门关》 the opera *Yanmen Pass*

Yanyang Lou 《艳阳楼》 the opera *Yanyang Tower*

Yao Qi 《姚期》 the opera *General Yao Qi*

Yingxiong yi 英雄衣 another name for *bao* jackets and trousers (literally, "heroes' clothes")

Yu Guoyuan 《御果园》 the opera *The Imperial Orchard*

Yu Tangchun 《玉堂春》 the opera *Courtesan Yu Tangchun*

yuanbao lian 元宝脸 ingot-pattern face, a design of facial makeup

yueqin 月琴 four-stringed moon-shaped Chinese mandolin

Zeng Tipao 《赠绨袍》 the opera *Gift of a Silk Robe*

Zha Mei An 《铡美案》 the opera *The Execution of Chen Shimei*

Zhan Taiping 《战太平》 the opera *The Taiping War*

Zhan Wancheng 《战宛城》 the opera *The Battle of Wancheng*

Zhen Tanzhou 《镇潭州》 the open *Conquering Tanzhou*

zhengdan 正旦 "chief dan," another name for *qingyi*

zhengjing 正净 primary painted-face role

zhenglian 整脸 full-facial makeup

zhengsheng 正生 "respectable man," another term for *laosheng*

zhezi 褶子, or *xuezi* as it is popularly known to people in theatrical circles, robe that overlaps at the front

Zhi Qu Weihu Shan 《智取威虎山》 the modern opera *Taking Tiger Mountain by Strategy*

zhong 钟 bell

Zhuo Fang Cao 《捉放曹》 the opera *The Capture and Release of Cao Cao*

zoushui 走水 an embroidered three-layer silk skirt at the bottom of a *bao* jacket

图书在版编目（CIP）数据

国粹：中国京剧 / 易边编著.－北京：外文出版社，2005
ISBN 978-7-119-03697-7

I. 国… II. 易… III. 京剧－基本知识－英文
IV.J821

中国版本图书馆 CIP 数据核字（2004）第 043472 号

策　　划　肖晓明
责任编辑　胡开敏　雷喜红
英文翻译　张韶宁
英文编辑　Peter Brenan　郁　苓
装帧设计　宁成春　陈　嘉
印刷监制　张国祥

本书图片得到北京梅兰芳纪念馆、中国艺
术研究院以及刘占文先生、谭元杰先生、兰
佩瑾先生等支持，特此鸣谢！

国粹——中国京剧

易 边 编

*

© 外文出版社
外文出版社出版
（中国北京百万庄大街 24 号）
邮政编码　100037
外文出版社网址 http://www.flp.com.cn
外文出版社电子信箱: info@flp.com.cn ; sales@flp.com.cn
北京京都六环印刷厂 印刷
中国国际图书贸易总公司发行
（中国北京车公庄西路 35 号）
北京邮政信箱第 399 号　邮政编码　100044
2005 年(大 20 开)第 1 版
2007 年第 1 版第 2 次印刷
（英）
ISBN 978-7-119-03697-7/G · 787（外）
09800
7-E-3620 P